Ellis Island
Welcome to America

Marcus Figorito

The Rosen Publishing Group's
READING ROOM
Collection: Social Studies™
New York

Published in 2006 by The Rosen Publishing Group, Inc.
29 East 21st Street, New York, NY 10010

Copyright © 2006 by The Rosen Publishing Group, Inc.

Book Design: Ron A. Churley

Photo Credits: Cover (front), p. 1 © Bob Krist/Corbis; Cover (back) © Gail Mooney/Corbis; pp. 4–5 © Donald L. Miller/International Stock; pp. 6–7 by Ron A. Churley; pp. 8, 11, 12, 14 © Hulton Archive/Archive Photo; p. 9 © SuperStock; pp. 10–11 (inset) © Catholic University of America, Department of Archives, Manuscripts, and Museum Collections.
ISBN: 1-4042-3347-4

Library of Congress Cataloging-in-Publication Data

Figorito, Marcus.
Ellis Island : welcome to America / Marcus Figorito.
p. cm. – (The reading room collection. Social studies) Includes index.
ISBN 1-4042-3347-4 (library binding)
1. Ellis Island Immigration Station (N.Y. and N.J.)–History–Juvenile literature. 2. United States–Emigration and immigration–History–Juvenile literature. I. Title. II. Rosen Publishing Group's reading room collection. Social studies.
JV6484.F54 2006

2005011884

Manufactured in the United States of America

Contents

Today, people visit Ellis Island to learn about the history of immigration to America.

Welcome to America!

Ellis Island is in New York Harbor between the states of New Jersey and New York. For sixty-two years, it was a place that welcomed **immigrants** coming to the United States. Today it is part of the **Statue of Liberty** National Monument. Just like the Statue of Liberty, Ellis Island stands for American **freedom**.

The Early History of Ellis Island

Ellis Island had many owners over the years. Dutch and English fishermen once gathered **oysters** there. A store owner named Samuel Ellis bought the land in the 1770s and gave the island its present name.

Original island showing Fort Gibson buildings

Ellis Island today

Between 1808 and 1812, the U.S. government built Fort Gibson on the island to help guard New York City during the **War of 1812**.

The original island was only 3.3 acres. The U.S. government increased the size of the island to 27.5 acres.

Doorway to America

In 1890, President Benjamin Harrison decided to turn Ellis Island into a U.S. immigration station. Between 1892 and 1954, over 12 million

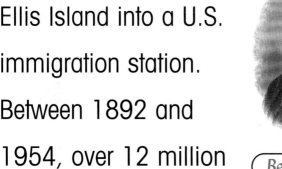

Benjamin Harrison

immigrants passed though Ellis Island before entering the United States. These people hoped to find a better life in America, since life was often very hard in their own countries.

 The immigration station at Ellis Island was opened in 1892, but was destroyed by a fire in 1897. The station was rebuilt and opened again in December 1899.

Becoming an American Citizen

Each immigrant was questioned before entering America. The U.S. government made sure immigrants were able to work to make money for their families. Doctors looked at each immigrant to make sure they were healthy. After passing through Ellis Island, immigrants moved to many different places in the United States.

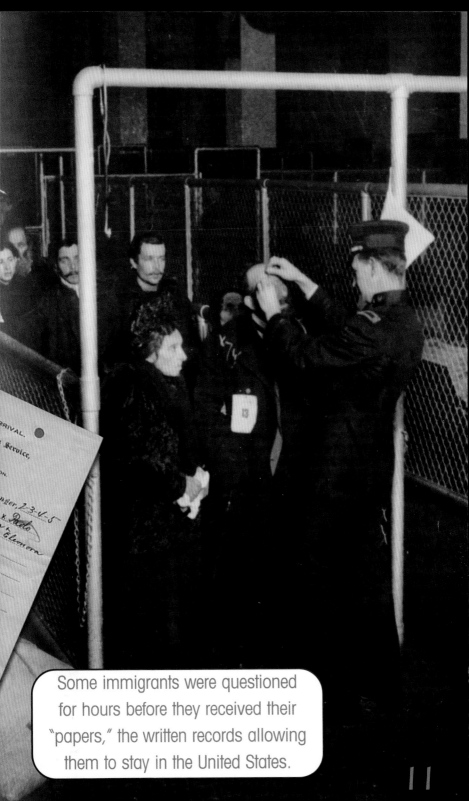

Some immigrants were questioned for hours before they received their "papers," the written records allowing them to stay in the United States.

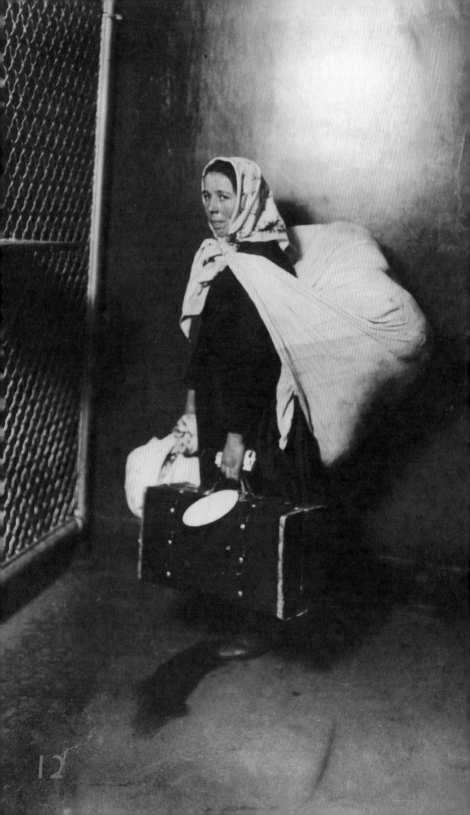

12

The Fear of Immigration

Some Americans began to fear that immigrants would change the country. New laws set **quotas** (KWOH-tuhz) that allowed only a certain number of immigrants from each country to enter the United States. As a result, fewer people came to America. After 1924, very few people went through Ellis Island to enter America. In 1954, Ellis Island was closed down.

In 1907, over 1.25 million immigrants—like the woman shown here—came through Ellis Island.

A Sign of American Freedom

In 1965, President Lyndon Johnson made Ellis Island part of the Statue of Liberty National Monument. In 1990, the main building was reopened as a **museum**. About 2 million people visit Ellis Island every year. Many people

Lyndon Johnson

go to see the "Wall of Honor," which shows the names of over 600,000 immigrants. Ellis Island has become a lasting sign of American freedom.

Glossary

freedom   The power to do, say, or think as you please.

immigrant   A person who moves to a new country from another country.

museum   A building people can visit to see art or historical objects.

oyster   An ocean animal with a hard shell.

quota   A limited number of people from a larger group.

Statue of Liberty   A monument in New York Harbor south of Ellis Island. France gave the statue to the United States in 1884.

War of 1812   A war between the United States and England that lasted from 1812 to 1815.

Index